Tales From

LaMPLIGHT Lane

Book 3

PLUTOPIa

Darren S. Philibert

WP

Whimsical Publications, LLC

Florida

Tales from Lamplight Lane: Plutopia is a work of fiction. Names, characters, and incidents are the products of the author's imagination and are either fictitious or are used fictitiously. Any resemblance to actual events or persons, living or dead, is entirely coincidental.

To purchase the authorized electronic edition of
Tales from Lamplight Lane: Plutopia, visit
www.whimsicalpublications.com

Cover art by Janet Durbin
Editing by Brieanna Robertson

ISBN-13: 978-1-63495-032-9

Published by
Whimsical Publications, LLC
Florida

acknowledgement

For Pluto (the planet not the dog)

DEDICATION:

This book is dedicated to the interesting, and many times contradictive, English language. What other language allows you to drive on a parkway and park on a driveway? And where the word "phonetic" is not spelled the way it sounds. It's a language all its own in the fact that it's both unique and vexing. For example, some common words we use on a daily basis are not at all English, but rather borrowed from another language because someone was just too lazy to come up with an English word for it on their own. Such as coupon; an old French term meaning "piece cut off." Which, now that I think about it, two-for-one-coupon does sound a whole lot better than two-for-one piece cut off.

Another brilliant attribute is the silent letter, such as the "P" in pneumonia or the "O" in Opossum, that apparently have no other purpose than to generally annoy the populous and to stifle elementary school spelling bee contestants. And can someone tell me why most people will say the word orange just fine by itself, but if you add juice to the end of it, it suddenly becomes "Ornch?" Any way you look at it, English is the mutt of languages, with borrowed words, silent letters, and confusion mixed in a big pot, stirred and poured into your brains by your second grade teacher Ms. Fullerton.

Now that that has been said, I hope you enjoy the story and I promise I will try my best not to include any words with silent letters, so as not to upset you.

...Oh, and archeology, it's dedicated to archeology too.

TABLE OF CONTENTS

a KooKY case WITH a HeaDLess cHase

The sound of four-pawed feet pounding on the old cobbled road echoed down the empty street. The Great Dane ran with his huge tongue flopping out of his mouth. Clyde stopped to catch his breath. He looked back and saw the moon low in the sky. Then, breaking the horizon, was a figure on a horse black as pitch. It reared in the air. Its rider was dressed all in black with riding gloves and boots. A ragged cape floated behind him with a tall pointed collar that circled around where normally a head would be. The headless horseman galloped off in hasty pursuit after the dog, brandishing a black steel sword that matched his ensemble. Clyde started running again, seeing his goal just up ahead. The bridge. Once passing through it, he would be safe. (Now, I know what you're thinking. How could the headless horseman be in Lamplight Lane? He is the legend of Sleepy Hollow. I agree, but tell that to the headless chap currently chasing Clyde on horseback). He was almost there. He just had to run into the covered bridge. He could hear the horse's hooves clopping on the road behind him getting closer and closer.

Standing on top of the covered bridge was Francis,

Ralf, Palyn, and Waddles. Francis went over his plan once more with the others. "So when the horseman stops at the bridge, we all throw this net over top him and we'll have him!" They were all ready.

They saw Clyde running as a Great Dane down the street with the headless horseman right on his tail, almost literally. Clyde ran into the bridge, barking as he did so. The horseman stopped at the bridge, swinging his sword in anger. Francis yelled, "Now!" and they all threw the net.

As they threw the net, Waddles lost his balance and fell off the roof of the bridge, but managed to land in a branch of a tree next to it. Because of this, the net fell short and missed the horseman. The horseman's horse reared on its hind legs and turned to gallop off. Just then the branch Waddles had landed on started cracking. The branch broke and Waddles fell. The horseman never saw it coming.

The gang came running over to the scene and saw Waddles sitting on top of the headless horseman, who was down for the count.

Just then Sheriff Mooney pulled up. "Hey now, what's all this?" he asked.

"This," said Francis, "is the end of the mystery. Now let's see who the headless horseman really is." Francis reached down, pulled off the cape and heightened shoulder pads, and revealed a very disgruntled-looking woman.

"Rooby Roo!" shouted Clyde.

"That's right, Clyde," said Francis. "It's Ruby Rew, the mastermind behind this whole operation."

"But how could that be, Fancis?" asked Palyn. "We saw Ruby at the same time we saw the horseman."

"With some clever use of wires, a projector, and some sound effects played over a loud speaker, she made it seem like the place was terrorized by a headless horseman and scared people away from her illegal gold smuggling operation in the town's abandoned caves."

"And I would have gotten away with it too if it wasn't for you meddling kids and that dog!" shouted Ruby.

"Wait a minute," said Ralf. "Where is Professor Copperpot? We never found him." The entire gang looked at Ruby, but she turned her head with a defiant look.

"Don't worry, gang. I think I know where to find him," said Francis. After a few minutes, they were all in the old abandoned cave. Just inside there was an old shack. Francis opened door and there inside was Professor Silas Copperpot, tied and gagged. They quickly untied him.

"Thanks, kids. I thought I would never see the light of day again," said a relieved Professor Copperpot.

"Any time, professor," said Clyde.

Silas Copperpot
Born in Dead Horse, Alaska, Silas and his family moved to Las Vegas, New Mexico when he was only 2 years old (not to be confused with Las Vegas, Nevada, which is much more exciting than their small boring town). His father, an accomplished circus performer, was known as Cannonball Copperpot. Although he performed many daring and dangerous stunts for the circus, he was most well-known for his human cannonball stunts. Silas also had a brother that was very much into exploring and history, but young Chester's story is told elsewhere.

One fateful day, Cannonball Copperpot was to be shot across a wide well-known river. The entire town showed up for the stunt. Copperpot rocketed out of the cannon with great precision and grace, but right about at the midway point, he swallowed a large June bug (ironically in the month of June) and choked in mid-air, and was dead before he hit the other side.

That same day the funeral was held, it was decided that the casket holding Cannonball Copperpot would be fired out of a cannon into Conchas Lake; it would be Cannonball Copperpot's last performance. Right before the cannon was to fire, a June bug flew over and landed on a rather large woman who was standing very close to the cannon and scared the dickens out of her!. She panicked, arms flailing, and bumped into the cannon, knocking the stabilizer loose so that the cannon rotated and aimed straight up (it seems the June bugs still had it out for Silas' father). It went off and shot Cannonball Copperpot strait up into the air. After a few moments, needless to say, the casket came rocketing back to earth and landed with a crash some 200 feet away. Upon arriving at the crash site, it appeared that the casket had broken through into some kind of cavern. Silas was the first to scurry down the hole and reach the bottom. The casket had burst apart when crashing through the cavern roof and the corpse of Silas' father dangled in the arms of a giant stone statue of unknown origin. Silas stood there in absolute shock. He had never seen a more amazing statue. So, on the day of his father's death, his love for archeology was born.

Professor Copperpot had been missing for weeks, right around the time the headless horseman started galloping about the town. Silas spit out the cloth pieces that remained in his mouth and excitedly told the kids, "Have I got news for you. I have discovered something very intriguing."

2

IN YOUR FACE, COPERNICUS!

"It all started one evening when I was peering through my Telephonscope.* I was spending a relaxing evening gazing around the heavens when I spotted the Lamplight Lane Satellite. Upon closer examination, I saw something that took my breath away. Sticking out of the clumps of rock below the orbital town, just barely visible, was what appeared to be the ruins of a city, completely upside down. I couldn't believe my eyes. I had to find out what it was and how it came to be. I immediately began to make preparations for an expedition to the subterranean depths below Lamplight Lane. Thinking that my best bet for getting down to this city was through the town's abandoned mining caves, I sought them out. That is where I ran into the headless horseman and wound up tied up in this old shack. I guess Ruby figured I was on to her little operation. But, in fact, I knew nothing about it. I can see that you kids are clever lads. I could use someone like you fellas on my exploration, what do ya say?"

"We wouldn't miss it for anything, Professor Copperpot," answered Francis. The rest of the boys all chimed in with their agreement, except for Waddles who had just swallowed a June bug.

*Telephonscope: An invention by Professor Sigmund Rubic that is a telescope with a built-in telephone. This allows the stargazer to be able to be the first to contact the local Astronomy Department, in case they spot a new celestial body, so as to have first discovery and it named after them. It also is handy for ordering pizza on those long, boring, uneventful nights of observation.

3

SPELUNKING IS FUN TO SAY

    After returning home to gather supplies and equipment, each of the boys met professor Copperpot back at the mine entrance before they set off. Soon they were winding their way down the old dark caves, each with a lantern to light their way. Deeper and deeper they went until they came to an elevator shaft that dropped down into a pit of pitch blackness. On the wall next to it was an old electric box with a large toggle switch on it. Professor Copperpot went to the box and flipped the switch up with a clunk. A few lights nearby came on while others flickered or never came on at all. He then went over to the elevator controls and pressed a green recessed button. It made a buzzing noise when pushed and a metal clanking noise could be heard down the shaft. After a few minutes, an elevator cart came up and stopped at the top. Silas opened up the chain link gate and waved his arm inward. "All aboard."

    The old metal cage rattled and groaned as it descended down the dark pit. It seemed they went on for miles, and the heat started to grow. Finally, they reached the bottom and exited the elevator. The tunnel in which they found themselves had been built by a machine, by the looks of the walls. They were very smoothly ground. Then, after following it for a while, they came to a section where the smooth tunnel stopped, but then a smaller, more crudely chiseled one began. They went single file down the primitive shaft that wound downward for what seemed hours. Emerging, they came into a bigger opening in the cave with stalagmites and stalactites jutting here and there like the mouth of a ravenous Larpbeast. What's a Larpbeast, you ask? It's a beast with a mouth that looks like the cave I just described...please stay with me.

Silas decided to rest here and have a bite to eat. As they sat around eating egg salad sandwiches Francis' mom made for them, Silas entertained them with a story from one of his many exciting archeological digs.

*Spelunking – Although fun to say, is the recreational sport of exploring caves.

4

LOST aND FOUND IN TranSLaTION

"The year is 1922. The place is the Valley of the Kings, Egypt, on the west bank of the Nile River across from Thebes. Archeologist Howard Carter and his team discover the tomb of an ancient Pharaoh named Tutankhamen, or better known as King Tut. I had nothing to do with this dig. I just wanted to get your blood stirring for adventure. Now, don't worry, I have a great story to tell about how I was involved in a great archeological find. It was the 70s, 1974 to be exact. Bell bottoms, massive sideburns, and wide brown-striped ties ruled the scene, and I had all three. I also coined the phrase 'Can you dig it?' by being overheard talking to my assistant about a dig site on a pay phone on the streets of Harlem. And, before it was popular slang, it was also common among the scientific community to ask if they were an archeologist by simply saying 'you dig?'

"I had decided to backpack China and sight-see the beautiful countryside. In a province called Shaanxi, I ran across some local farmers in an old pick-up truck. From the little Chinese I had learned from a small pocket translator book, I hitched a ride with them. When they came to their work site where they were going to drill a new water well, I attempted to wish them luck by saying, 'I hope you find much water today.' However, the foreman must have misunderstood me (because my Chinese was spot on) and thought I said, 'I heard your wife's water broke today.' It just so happened that his wife was pregnant. The man panicked and jumped into the truck and tore off for the town a few miles away.

"Now the rest of the farmers didn't know where to drill now that the foreman was gone, so they proceeded to drill where they figured he wanted them to. Soon thereafter, they made the amazing discovery of the 8,000 Terracotta Army stone statues of the first emperor of Qin: Shi Huang. Even though they never credited me for helping them with the find, I know that if I had not been misunderstood, they never would have found those statues, and thus history made. I always thought it interesting how you can make history by finding history. I guess some things are so great that they can become historic more than once.

"Archeology is a fickle business."

5

a river runs upside-Down Through it

After listening to Silas and his experiences, the gang understood more about who Silas Copperpot was. That and probably why he got the nickname of Silas Crackpot. They gathered their belongings and set off once more down the rocky cave system.

One by one, their lanterns died out until it was down to just the one lantern that Silas carried. They hurried as fast as they could. They soon came upon an underground river. Silas told them that it had to flow somewhere and they best follow it. Along the river they came to a section where the water pooled and sat for a quick drink. Suddenly, Ralf yelled at the others to come look at something. They all came over and shined the lantern on a most curious sight. The river ended in a waterfall. Now I know that a waterfall is no special phenomena, but what about one that fell upwards?

The river just started flowing up a few rocks then simply fell up to the ceiling and started a new river that flowed along the roof of the cave. The whole group watched it with mouths and eyes open wide. Clyde reached out into the backwards waterfall and drank some. They all looked at him. "What? I just wanted to see what a reverse waterfall tastes like."

As they continued down the cave, they started to notice that the river on the ceiling now started to run along the wall then slowly came back down and ran along their feet. "Well that was definitely strange, it's like the river can't make up its mind whether it wants to run along the floor or the ceiling," noted Francis.

"Actually, I believe the river is still running along the ceiling," said Silas. "And it is us who has in fact changed, not the river." They looked at him as if he just blown a head gasket.

"Say what, Professor?" said Clyde.

"Remember, the city I saw was upside-down, so it must be some strange gravitational anomaly. It just seemed to us that the river started flowing back down the wall, but it was us that were actually walking up the wall to meet *it*."

They continued their trek, and not too long after, their last light died.

"What do we do now, Silas?" asked Francis.

"Don't worry, my boy, we will just continue to follow the river," said Silas. Suddenly, lights burst to life all around them. It blinded them, since their eyes were used to the dark already. As their eyes adjusted, they saw the source of the light. They were torches held by strange-looking people. They all wore big, round welding goggles and grey jumpsuits. They looked human except for the fact that had a grey-green complexion, stout stocky bodies, and white hair.

"Sweet!" exclaimed Ralf. "Molemen!"

6

∩ ∪ i a ∪?

One of the creatures who appeared to be the leader stepped forward and said, "Surrender or die."

They all looked at each other. Then Silas said, "We did not mean to disturb you, we are just peaceful explorers and were curious about what was down here. We want to learn about your culture and your society as friends."

"Tell us then, overlanders, are you from the International Astronomical Union*?" said the leader.

They all thought that a very strange question indeed. "No, we are not," answered Silas.

"Oh...well then...you are welcome among us. My name is Floydd Withtoodees."

Clyde had a puzzled look on his face and asked, "So is your last name Withtoodees? Or is your first name actually spelled with two D's?

"My last name is Withtoodees...but now that you mention it, my first name is also spelled with two D's... Funny, I never noticed that before," said Floydd Withtoodees in a spacey kinda way. "Anywho, if you follow us, we will provide you with food and a place to stay while you are on your visit. And stop by our souvenir shop for some great t-shirts for 50% off while supplies last." He then told them to follow them to the city.

*The International Astronomical Union (IAU) unites national astronomical societies from around the world. It also acts as the internationally recognized authority for assigning designations to celestial bodies (stars, planets, asteroids, etc.) and any surface features on them.

7

CITY UNDER WHERE?

After navigating through countless tunnels, they finally came to a vast cave at the top of a precipice. What they saw before them made their jaws drop (all except Waddles, who kept it shut while keeping a sharp lookout for June bugs). A large underground city sprawled out amongst the rocks and stalagmites. A beautiful sight. It had a strange contrast to it, with the old renaissance-looking city, but various types of technology here and there and strange devices equipped on various "mole-men."

"Welcome to Plutopia!" said the leader.

"Wow, Plutopia, that's a cool name," said Ralf.

"Well," said the leader "That was the top voted name of three."

"What were the other two?" asked Francis.

"Narnia and Middle Earth," said the leader

"Why Plutopia? Does it mean something?" asked Francis.

Floydd Withtoodees started speaking; all the other molemen started to bow their heads in silence and the lights dimmed for dramatic ambiance.

8

THE DAY A PLANET DIED

A poem by Floydd Withtoodees:

What a wonderful life, so spacious and free,
Floating in the heavens, with the entire universe to
see.
So old and timeless, I live on and on,
Here long before you were born, and will remain long
after you're gone.
Rank and status mean nothing to me,
For I am not concerned with social frivolity.
Yet self-proclaimed genius in the form of man,
Came to notice me through a glass-trimmed can.
They proceeded to acknowledge my existence with a
name.
Pluto, they said, and added me to their fame.
I did not care what these creatures said about me,
But as time passed on, I listened more intently.
They talked of my position in a system of sorts,
How it was taught to their young in schools, and writ-
ten in their reports.
I believed I was significant, important and great,

But soon would come, my humiliating fate.
The day then came when my status was revoked,
The outrage I felt, the anger it provoked.
Who were these men to treat me this way?
To raise me on a pedestal only to toss it away.

I never should have listened to their praise, and thrown myself into the mix.

I'll never forget the day I died, September thirteenth, two thousand and six.

9

aN aUDIeNCe WITH THe aNCIeNT ONe

Silas and the boys stood there with their heads downcast in respect. They all shed a tear for poor Pluto. Waddles also shed a tear, but for a different reason, because while engrossed in the story, he let down his guard and a June bug found its way down his throat. Out of all the bugs he has inadvertently swallowed in his life, they ranged on a scale of taste from horrible to not all that bad—this one rated an eight on the bad end of the spectrum.

Floydd Withtoodees then explained to them that if they had any more questions about their society, they were best off talking with their Ancient One, for he was the eldest of their people, and knew all things from their people's beginning. They agreed to see the Ancient One and had Floydd Withtoodees tell them how to get there. Floydd also pointed out they had a wonderful frozen yogurt hut near the pool if anyone was interested.

They walked through town past various Plutopian citizens, who gave them strange looks, and a few even hissed at them and scurried away as they passed by. Soon they approached a tall ziggurat that was at the northern most part of Plutopia. Here on the side of the ziggurat was a bronze plaque that read: PLEASE TAKE OFF YOUR SHOES, OR YOU'LL GET THE BOOT.

They all removed their footwear and proceeded to climb the tall staircase. Once they reached the top, they had a remarkable view of the entire city around them. Sitting cross-legged in the center on a large stone slab was a man with ripped jeans and Hawaiian shirt. His eyes were closed. He smiled and waved an arm. "Please sit." His eyes were still shut. With that, Silas and the boys sat around him cross-legged like he was. Even though he did not bid them to sit like him, they all felt it was just the proper thing to do. He was called the Ancient One, but he didn't look over 30 years of age. "Shall I speak?" he asked.

They looked at each other, thinking it odd that he asked them that.

"Yes of course," said Silas. "We would like to hear what you have to say."

"It's not a matter of liking it or not; if I say it, you will hear it. You can't very well hear what I have not said," said the Ancient One.

"Er...yes...that's true enough," said Silas. "Please go on then."

The Ancient One cleared his throat, picked his nose, and began his tale. All the while never once opening his eyes.

10

THE TALE OF EDISON: THE WHALE THAT HAD IRIDESCENT LIGHTBULBS FOR EYES

"As we all know, (or at least I hope you all know), all whales are mammals, live in the ocean, and have eyes. Our eyes allow us to see everything...well, almost everything. For no one can see past the physical appearance of another. No one except Edison. Edison, you see, was a whale, a whale that had a unique ability to see the innermost feelings of other creatures. And what allowed him to do this, you ask? He had iridescent lightbulbs for eyes. No one knows exactly how having iridescent lightbulb eyes allows one to see the emotional status of another, but here is my theory. "Lightbulbs allow us to see things in a clear light. They expose what was once in darkness and open them to examination and understanding. Iridescence is an optical phenomenon in which hue changes with the angle from which a surface is viewed, allowing the viewer to see the view-ee in various different lights and aspects. So nothing is viewed from a single perspective, but rather is in a constant state of flux. So for Edison, instead of regular old run-of-the-mill eyes that only see the outward appearance, he very clearly saw various angles of a person's being.

"Amazing as Edison's ability was, he was not looked upon by admiring eyes. Most of the other sea creatures looked disdainfully at him, calling him names and viewing him as a freak. But Edison could see the real reasons why they made fun of him. Most were jealous, and others were scared of what was unusual. Other whales who knew him best would call him names and teasingly ask him how he slept at night. Life with lightbulbs for eyes was a burden for poor Edison, and everyone made sure to remind him of this.

"After a day of excessive jeering and jesting at Edison's expense, he decided to take a swim to a peaceful area where he could be alone with his thoughts. Edison was so depressed that he grew angry at himself, cursing the eyes that he had, seeing them as a burden rather than a gift. He made a decision. He would rather be blind than have this burden any longer. He spotted a large rock a few meters out and decided to swim at full speed, crash into the rock, break his lightbulb eyes, and rid him of this curse once and for all.

"Edison lined himself up and shot towards the rock like a bullet. As he approached at great speed, he suddenly saw something that made him twist at the last moment and avoid the blinding collision. This rock was no rock. It was another whale! Edison turned around and examined it, which he found to be female. She was lying there, presumably dead. Her eyes were closed and she wasn't moving. Edison could detect a very faint feeling from her of deep sadness, loneliness, and abandonment. But even more interesting was a large metal panel of sorts formed to her back that ran from head to tail.

"Edison floated above her, intrigued, and curious to take a closer look at the panel. Suddenly, a few tiny lights started to flash on the panel and she began to move and open her eyes. Under closer scrutiny, Edison saw that they were solar panels that his eyes had apparently charged and brought life to the slumbering whaless. Slowly, she looked up at Edison as a smile grew on her lips. 'Thank you,' she said weakly. She tilted her head thoughtfully and added, 'You have such beautiful eyes.'

"Edison now saw that the she-whale's sadness and loneliness was fading, being replaced with happiness and contentment. The more she smiled at him, the more brightly his eyes shone, charging her panels and giving life to her smile. It was the perfect circle of symbiosis. As they swam off together, Edison then understood that they were, quite literally, made for each other."

11

where's ziggurat?

The Ancient One sat there in silence after the story had ended, eyes still closed, and Silas and the boys looked at each other, wondering if he was going to speak again. He did not.

"Well that was a very nice story, indeed, but what does that have to do with your people's history?" asked Silas

"Nothing," said The Ancient One.

"Well, can you now tell us about your people's history?" asked Silas.

"You'll want to talk to the Ancient One for that," said the person they formerly thought was the Ancient One.

"You're not the Ancient One?" asked Francis.

"Nope, the name's Ed. The Ancient One is on the other Ziggurat across town."

"Oh, I'm terribly sorry. We must have got turned around. Well, thanks for the story; it was riveting! But we must be going now," said Silas.

"Very well then, Uop-camf-mt-wbayb," said Ed.

"I'm sorry, what was that?" asked Silas.

Ed heaved a great irritated sigh. "It's short for 'until

our paths cross again, my friend, may the wind be at your back.' But it completely negates the convenience of it if you have to explain it." Ed jumped up and stormed off the other side of the ziggurat, obviously offended.

12

POP POP, FIZZ FIZZ, OH WHAT a RELIEF, WE ARE FINALLY AT THE ANCIENT ONE'S ZIGGURAT

Twelve blocks, four yogurt shop stops, and two incomprehensible Waddle travesties later, (involving a Rickshaw, a firework stand, and a portable mp3 player with a short in it, thus creating a kind of out of control rocket car) they reached the Ancient One's ziggurat in one piece, albeit slightly singed.

They all proceeded to climb the ziggurat, when all of a sudden...actually, I think I'll go back and explain what happened with the rocket car, it's very entertaining.

After Waddles stopped at the fourth yogurt vendor along the way, the boys were curious as to why there were so many yogurt shops here. They found the procurator (a fancy word for owner) of the shop and asked him. He pointed outside to a tall stalagmite in a large pool of water with another upside down flowing waterfall that disappeared into a large opening in the ceiling. On top of that stalagmite was a white truck with the words "Jolly Roger's Ice Cream" printed on the side. He explained that long ago, when they first arrived here, that truck was their sole source for food for a short time.

Thus, it became the life-giver of the newly subterranean people. They revered it as a savior and it became an icon of sustenance.

As he was explaining all this to the Silas and the boys, Waddles' attention was caught by a rickshaw and he went over to take a look. The rickshaw driver was placidly listening to music when Waddles' yogurt-cone dripped down onto the poor man's mp3 player, which made it short-circuit and start to spark. The startled man dropped the mp3 player, but the wire attached to the headphones had been run under his shirt and into his ears. He tried to get away from the sparking music device and ran headlong into a firework stand. The resulting collision erupted into a brilliant colorful display seen all over the city. Several fireworks shot outward, hitting the ice cream truck, toppling it over and into the large pool with a splash. In just a matter of moments, the Jolly Roger's Ice Cream Truck swirled around like a Hotwheels in a toilet and was sucked up the reverse waterfall and into the chasm in the ceiling, going who-knows-where. Whilst everyone's attention was captured by the fireworks and the desecration of the iconic truck, Waddles quietly slipped away, licking the yogurt off his sticky hand.

Now back to the story...

They all proceeded to climb up the ziggurat when, all of a sudden, they were at the top! Sorry, that was so anti-climactic (fancy word for nothing at all exciting happened), but it's simply what happened. They were greeted there by a not-so-old looking man. He had a large grin and jumped up to greet them, shaking each one's hand in turn.

"Hullo, hullo, I'm known as the Ancient One. Come, come, sit, relax. Can I interest you in some iced tea?"

The boys and Silas looked a little taken back.

"S-sure, thank you," stammered Silas.

The Ancient One walked over to a little cooler, pulled out a pitcher of iced tea, and gave them each a cup. "Well now," he said. "You don't look like you're from around here. Have you just arrived?"

"Yes, we came from the town of Lamplight Lane many miles above you," answered Francis.

At the mention of the name of the town, the Ancient One's eyes glazed over as if reliving some old disturbing memory. "The horror," he whispered. "The horror."

"I'm sorry, does that bring back some bad memories?" asked Silas

"Hunh? What?" said the Ancient One, snapping out of it. "Oh no, no, no, sorry I just realized I'm out of ice to put in your drinks. Now how can I be a proper host without ice for you drinks? Oh well. You're the first of the overworlders to come down here. Now what can I, the Ancient One, do for you fine folk this day?"

"We were hoping you could tell us of your civilization and how you came to be down here?" asked Silas.

"Ah yes, many have wondered that, and come here seeking my great wisdom and knowledge of our history," he said with a prideful smile.

"But I thought you said we were the first to come here?" said Ralf.

"Please don't interrupt me, young man, it's very rude. Now where was I? Oh yes, the history of our people...can I interest any of you in this t-shirt with a clever little anecdote on the front?" The shirt he held up said: *I climbed up the Ancient One's ziggurat looking for infinite wisdom and all I got was this lousy shirt.* "Its 50% off, while supplies last."

13

THE e-ProPHeCY

"It all started on a Thursday, much like any other Thursday. The air was still like it always is here, being underground and all. Most people were out and about with their daily activities. Then at one precise moment, the city of Plutopia was filled with beeps, chimes, and alerts of all types from a massive text and email sent to every cell phone, PDA, and Laptop in the city. After the echo faded, it was as if time stood still. Everyone paused with jaw-dropping shock. We, the people of Plutopia, had received the E-prophecy of Pluto's return, and it read like this:

Dearest sons and daughters, I beith the one you hath referred to as Pluto. My time for rebirth is nigh. Soon you wilst behold me cometh to you in great glory. I sendith this massive text to inform you of the signs giving thou proof that my time for return is here.

Sign #1: Strangers from the Overworld will visit you.

Sign #2: All t-shirts will go on sale at 50% off.

Sign #3: The great provider will be removed from its pedestal and ascend to the unknown.

Sign #4: Pestilence on a massive scale

Once these signs hath been revealed, looketh to the heavens, for I have cometh!

"And ever since your arrival here, all of those signs have come to pass, all except the fourth."

Just then Waddles, who was so engrossed with the story, took a sip of his iced tea but miscalculated and poured it down his head instead of his mouth. Blind from the tea streaming down his face, he reached for the nearest cloth, which happened to be Payln's cloth bag. After removing it to wipe his wet face, Payln tried to grab back the cloth, but inadvertently knocked Waddles over, who fell into a small control panel of sorts that turned on a camera system (this was used by the Ancient One to broadcast to the city any important information involving city planning, prophecy updates, and red tag sales). Once activated, the entire city had front row seats to the most gut-wrenching sight on Earth. Hurling erupted on a massive scale the likes of which none had ever seen.

After Payln got his bag back over his horrible head, the Ancient One took control of the cameras. He made a city-wide announcement.

"Dear citizens of Plutopia, I have good news and bad news. The good news is the final sign has been revealed to us! The bad news is, the city street sweeper is broken down and won't be up and running till next week."

14

PLUTO OFF THE PORT BOW!

Just then, the phone rang and the Ancient One picked it up. "Uh huh, ya, uh huh, ya, mhm, ya, okay." The Ancient One hung up the phone. "They have Pluto on the Telephonescope. Come, let us go take a look at Pluto's glorious return." He ran past them and down the ziggurat's stairs, the boys and Silas fast on his heels.

They arrived at a tall watchtower and climbed the winding staircase to the top. Bursting through a door on the roof, they walked over to a man standing next to extremely long telephonescope that rose for a few hundred feet and ended just below a stone circle opening in the ceiling of the cavern. The opening was the bottom of a very deep well that was just outside Lamplight near the Libretary. So through it, they could gaze upon the stars.

The Ancient One looked though the telephonescope and stared in silent awe. He beckoned the others to come look and see Pluto's return for themselves. Silas especially was very curious about this. After peering into the telephonescope, he saw something that both shocked and relieved him. It was not Pluto he was looking at, but was indeed the orbital Lamplight Lane. Silas turned away from the telephonescope and looked to the Ancient One. Before he could even get a single syllable out, a form materialized out of thin air next to him, grabbed Silas, and both vanished back into, I assume thin air, from which he had come.

15

circular logic

Silas opened his eyes to everything the exact way it had been, except for two things. The boys were gone and Professor Rubic was now there along with most of the city's population. He still stood on top of the Ancient One's ziggurat in Plutopia. He looked at Rubic. "Professor! How...what's..." Silas couldn't make his brain wrap around the strange events.

"Don't fret, Mr. Copperpot, all will be explained," assured Rubic.

Silas turned when the Ancient One cleared his throat behind him."Hello, Mr. Copperpot, welcome back to Plutopia," said the Ancient One.

"Back?" asked Silas.

"Yes, we are actually from the future...but are currently in the present."

"So... I must be on the Orbital Lamplight Lane..."

"Indeed you are. Allow me to explain the events that you have recently witnessed. Here, have some yogurt while you listen."

THE ANCIENT ONE'S STORY OF WHAT THE HECK IS

GOING ON:

"Many moons ago in September of two thousand and six, there was a heresy of sorts in the scientific community. We lost a beloved heavenly body to a second-rate category. A large group of us protested but were shunned by the others. We were driven out of said community and so we retreated underground. At first just to find a neat place to play a game of Dungeons and Dragons, but then we stumbled upon the old city deep underground. We then knew that we had found our new home, where we could plot our revenge on the scientific community and thus get Pluto back where he belonged. Yet, all of our attempts were fruitless. Letter after stern letter, they paid no heed to our petitions. We had all but given up. Shortly thereafter, we did give up. But not long after that, a strange event occurred that rattled us. We were suddenly ripped up from the Earth and place among the stars. After having several long staff meetings about the event, and through the help of Professor Rubic (who supplies us with much of our technology) he apprised us of the situation. We then knew that we had become PLUTO REBORN! So it was now our duty to provide our past selves down on Earth with the inspiration that they would need so as not to give up hope in Pluto Reborn, and thus completing this whole circular prophecy thing. We then mass texted and emailed the self-fulfilling prophecy to everyone, and watched as events unfurled. So now they have Pluto back, and we have become Pluto Reborn for them. It all worked out pretty darn good, if you ask me."

Silas was dumbfounded by the story. He was both amazed and sick (apparently, the yogurt had given him indigestion).

Pushing through the crowd came the boys. "Sorry we missed your arrival, Silas, but we were buying t-shirts; they're 50% off, ya know."

"Quite all right, boys. Sorry, I'm just a bit dizzy from

all this," said Silas.

"So, Professor, we never did find out how this city came to be here, did we? Because it was found by the Plutopians, not built by them. I wonder who originally built it and lived here," asked Francis.

"That's true, Francis. It's possible we may never know. But we mustn't give up; we shall keep digging until we find an answer. I suggest we start searching Ed's ziggurat with our shoes *on*." Silas chuckled. "Are you with me, lads?"

"All the way, Silas," answered the boys.

"That's the spirit."

Silas and the boys set off down the steep steps of the ziggurat to solve the mysterious origins of the ancient city below Lamplight Lane. Waddles tripped on his shoelace (which was odd because he was wearing Velcro shoes) and tumbled the rest of the way down. Everyone laughed, including Waddles.

16

THE END OF THE BEGINNING

561 B.C

The earth shook with a tremendous tremor as a meteor roughly the size of New York City slammed into the ground, creating a dust cloud miles high. The alien rock embedded itself deep in the earth and, over the years, erosion melded it into our planet as its own. Six planets away sat a celestial body with a New York City-sized hole in it.

1280 A.D

Upon the same location in which the meteor had landed many years before, a king had built a castle and city out the very earth surrounding it. After the completion of the great city, the king held a ceremony celebrating the birth of his kingdom. Atop his ceremonial ziggurat, the king rose to make his speech to his people. The people cheered and praised him. He promised peace and prosperity and tunics at 50% off. After basking in the praise of his subjects, the king descended down the ziggurat and promptly tripped on his shoelace (which was odd because he was wearing royal slippers) and tumbled down the stairs, slamming into a giant pillar at the base. The pillar toppled over and crashed across the city well, opening up a fissure that caused a chain reaction that erupted into an earthquake that opened up the earth and swallowed the city whole. The few remaining people on the surface who escaped the cataclysmic event went crazy from seeing their city eaten up by the ground and ended up dwelling in huts and tents in the surrounding forest. The city, its inhabitants, and their beloved King Fedora that sank below were never heard from again.

About the Author

Darren S. Philibert

Darren Shawn Philibert has loved fantasy and adventure stories ever since his grandmother bought him the Chronicles of Narnia series by C.S Lewis when in middle school. His hobbies include reading (duh) board games and binge watching sci-fi shows. He lives in Eugene, Oregon with his book-loving wife Tara and their dorky cat Stormageddon (Stormy for short)

www.ingramcontent.com/pod-product-compliance
Lightning Source LLC
Chambersburg PA
CBHW020321150626
46552CB00022B/3070